Where Pigeons Roost

and other stories

A.M. Matte

Publications Nemesis

ISBN: 0992136504
ISBN-13: 978-0-9921365-0-5

CONTENTS

Acknowledgments   i

Abîme   1

Stalemate   10

Where Pigeons Roost   26

ACKNOWLEDGMENTS

Un gros merci to my family — Rohan, Jason, Alexandre, Lianne, Magali, Katia, Maman, Papa and Grand-Maman, whose support and encouragement are unending. Thanks to leilah vayid/See Sparks! for thoughtful and generous feedback and edits. Thanks to Maria Buscemi for her eye and her patience as she designed this book's cover, from a photograph by Alexandre Matte. Thanks to Sophie Tolias for the revisions, the camaraderie and the deadlines.

ABÎME

"You turn the key and push the door open, relieved to be home after a week-long book tour. The remodelled kitchen is impressive and you make a mental note to generously tip the contractor — until you see him, just around the corner, nestled in your wife's arms…"

She slams the book down with a huff. How dare he! To exploit their story is one thing; to misrepresent it is another. If anything, *she* was nestled in Eugenio's arms, not he in hers.

She rises briskly from the hideous tweed sofa overwhelming Eugenio's bachelor apartment. Had she known how much she would miss her own pristine, L-shaped, white leather reclining couch and king-sized bed, she may just have thought thrice before succumbing to his attentions.

And yet, was that all it was? She had to admit that there was just as much defiance and rebelliousness in her heart as there were stirrings and arousal in her loins when she first shared her bed with Eugenio. It wasn't so much about being with Eugenio as it was about not being with Drew. Forlorn hormones and frustration made it seem a justifiable step at the time.

It was Drew who'd accepted a last-minute book tour, even though she'd made a point of refusing all work that month so they could "spend more quality time together", as he put it. She'd even turned down the pilot for the action-adventure sitcom the public broadcaster was expecting would lead the fall lineup. (They'd eventually sweetened the offer and postponed shooting to accommodate her schedule, but she didn't know that at the time, did she?)

She feels like pacing, but there's no room. She squeezes around the sofa to the lone window of the apartment, perches on the ledge and watches people dash across the sidewalk to get out of the rain. She wishes she had somewhere to go.

Season Two shooting had wrapped on her feisty detective character three days ago. At the time, she longed for a break, just one moment away from the curious glances and obviously wagging tongues eager for any morsel of information to feed the gossip frenzy that her impending divorce had become. Seventy-two hours later, she yearns for those looks and whispers; the fuel keeping her career alive.

She fishes her iPhone out of her pocket and pulls up her favourite web pages: those about herself. One particularly devoted blogger has taken up her case. She finds comfort in this stranger's support: "*OMG people, leave the woman alone. We have so few authentically funny ladies to watch nowadays — who cares if she cheated?*"

Feeling lonely and abandoned save for a few dedicated fans, she returns to the sofa and picks up Drew's book, a thankfully short, thinly-veiled exposé of her affair, smooth and cool in her hands, yet containing a fiery account of her dalliance, sure to singe her public image.

"...*desolated and enraged by the betrayal, standing, as Potiphar must have, weighing consequence and feeling before uttering a deep growl: 'Get out.' You don't recognize your own voice. It is disembodied. It used to be jovial, trusting, naïve, loving.*

The contractor, with a quick nod, squeezes back into his white t-shirt — how could you not have noticed before how good-looking he is? — grabs his boots and exits so nonchalantly, you'd swear they were the couple bonded by vows. You stare at your bewildered wife, the rage and the shame of the cuckolded overtaking your urge to cry."

She stills her trembling hands and hazards a few pages further.

"*You drive aimlessly across town, your heartache growing exponentially and as wide as the billboards towering above, featuring your wife's pseudo-angelic face.*

You focus on the road, on the asphalt, on the white lines, on manoeuvring the car as a child would wield a crayon: your grip rigid on the wheel as you avoid the edges of the lane. Yet you can't block out the gnaw in your stomach, the vice on your lungs, the lump in your throat, and the insistent echo in your brain, the one

*you've been trying to drown out ever since you
left your house in a hollow daze: what did you
do to make her turn away from you, from
everything you've built together?"*

She looks up from the page and stares
blankly ahead for a moment before realizing
she has stopped breathing. She exhales slowly,
like she does in yoga — though she hasn't
attended any classes since the whole thing
began, the gym being in her former
neighbourhood, where she might run into Drew.

It hadn't occurred to her that Drew might
have felt anything but anger at her affair. The
cold and quiet way he'd left that night, the
courteous nod when she'd gone back to fetch
winter clothes, the clipped "It's best to transact
through our attorneys" text after her attempt to
reconcile. Even the note that accompanies the
proof of his book: "I thought it only fair to share
this with you before it goes public." No emotion,
no regret, no anguish. Not even a statutory
greeting — Drew is all business.

How much of what she holds in her
hands is fiction, as the front cover claims? She
knows most people will consider the novella a
pitch-perfect rendering of the truth, and that
public opinion — and sales — will be entirely in

Drew's favour. For her, this book, while vilifying her thoroughly, will at least ensure another season of her sitcom, whose producers will have apoplectic fits of joy at the added publicity and ratings it will bring to the show.

Yet, apart from a "fair" warning of what is ahead, is Drew not also reaching out to her? She allows herself hope that Drew, having put pen to paper, has reconsidered and is ready to, if not forgive her adultery, try and mend their relationship. "*What did you do to make her turn away from you?*"

She won't read the rest of the book. She doesn't want to let go of this feeling; foreign and familiar at the same time — an elation she could lose by scanning further. This is Drew's overture. She is sure of it, and won't allow herself to think otherwise. Could actual forgiveness come from the pages of a fictionalized story?

She pictures Drew in her mind's eye — dark-haired, bespectacled, a typical brooding writer, but with a crinkle in the corner of each eye, the only hints of a lightheartedness and joie de vivre, revealed to no one else but her. Until a year ago, when the light in Drew's eyes dimmed.

She imagines his homecoming differently:

"Honey, I'm home!" he'd say. (She forgives herself this cliché.)

She'd run to meet him in the foyer.

"Drew, you're early! I haven't finished making dinner, yet."

"How's my best girl?" He'd kiss her. "I take it the kitchen is done?"

"Yes, I gave the contractor the cheque today. Come see!"

He'd follow her to the brand-new, open-concept, islanded kitchen.

"It's well done. They did a good job," he'd say.

"Well done? It's gorgeous!"

"You know what's gorgeous? You in that apron. Makes me want to rip it off and ravish you right here. Christen the place, so to speak..."

He'd grab her and squeeze her close, his stout fingers grasping her buttocks and lifting her onto the slick marble countertop Eugenio had installed two days prior.

She sighs. She always does that. Her guilt inserts Eugenio into her reverie and she and Drew never consummate his return.

The initial, crazed, revenge-driven passion she shared with Eugenio is long gone. She insists on staying in his hovel; nothing to do with feelings for the contractor and everything to do with punishing herself by remaining with her one-time lover. Eugenio, not one to kick a beautiful woman out of his bed, stays away most nights, enjoying the unexpected and fruitful notoriety his reputation as a Lothario has brought him.

She glances around at the sparse apartment: the questionable décor, the inadequate bathroom, the barely-there kitchen. Why is she here?

Reading Drew's book, she finally realizes that her self-exile has caused her considerable harm. She thinks back to the night in question, when Drew left the house without a word. Rather than staying and facing the situation she'd created, she'd tracked down Eugenio and gone to him. By the time she'd returned, too many days later, and tried to explain herself to her husband, he was convinced she'd fallen in love with their contractor over tile samples and appliance specs. Her overtures had been dismissed.

But this book — Drew's book — fuels her hope that it may not be too late to reconcile.

Launching herself off the sofa and grabbing a hoodie, she dashes out, not bothering to lock the door behind her. Finding a subway token in her pocket, she makes her way home.

Drenched when she arrives, absorbed by visions of Drew's face and the feeling of his hair between her fingers, she barely notices that her soaked hoodie now holds more moisture than it blocks. She lowers her hood and smoothes out her hair, conscious of the closed-circuit camera they'd installed when they first moved in. She lifts the heavy lionhead door knocker and lets it drop. The thud reverberates through her as she fervently waits for Drew to answer the door.

STALEMATE

Ugh, how that backside exasperated her.

∞

In her contemplation, it didn't occur to
Feather that Gaelyn might feel equally irritated,
if not with her own backside, then some part of
Feather's physical aspect. Had she known then
the tumult that would follow, Feather may have
forgiven her sister her derrière and spent more
time pondering her own unrest. As for Gaelyn,
so much of her unfulfilled desires could be
resolved if she remembered the camaraderie
she'd once shared with Feather — but the
Hollingsworth sisters were not adept at self-
analysis. Despite their perceived dissimilarities,

10

Gaelyn and Feather shared the same fatal flaw: self-pity fraying their familial ties.

∞

Feather watched her sister bite into a scone as she laid the others upon the flowered platter, one by one. Why Gaelyn allowed herself this largesse was beyond her. Feather, at least, had maintained her svelte figure: she could bake the scones, but she wouldn't partake of them. If Gaelyn wanted to pad her buttocks, that was all very well; Feather didn't want to hear her squawk about it later.

The oven's bell dinged again.

"Could you hand me the potholder, please?"

Gaelyn held out her open palm, just out of Feather's reach, forcing Feather to rise from the kitchen chair from which she'd been polishing the silver teapot.

"You should have finished yesterday, you know," sniffed Gaelyn as she opened the oven door to check on the buns.

And then arose another of those increasingly common occasions during which Feather imagined Gaelyn's death. This time, she envisioned the impeccably timed hand of fate sending an insufficiently-chewed crumpet down Gaelyn's windpipe during that afternoon's tea, her face awash in several shades of blue as she clawed at her throat. Feather pictured the ladies uselessly squawking and fainting at the horror of their host's demise before the tea was poured: "If only she had taken a smaller bite..."

In her less gory imaginings, Feather simply wished Gaelyn would leave town and never return, leaving Feather to manage Hollingsworth Hall as she saw fit. She would open up their deceased parents' master suite and paint it turquoise. She would transform the kitchen from colonial to industrial. She might even remove the austere forest green drapes in the drawing room and replace them with a modern print.

Feather sighed.

"I was tired," she shrugged, hoping to avoid any further scolding.

Truth be told, she'd been distracted the day before. It was official. At the grocer's, she'd overheard that Jameson had finally proposed. So, that was that. Her former beau was engaged to Mabel's youngest sister, newly returned from nursing school. He wasn't a confirmed bachelor after all, just a very late-blooming groom-to-be.

Gaelyn might argue that an engagement — even a marriage — could be broken, but Feather no longer held any hope. Her dream of Jameson returning to her one day, perhaps even in old age, had long been dashed – not yesterday, if Feather dared admit it to herself, but rather when she first heard that Jameson was courting the youngest Deforest daughter.

∞

"They'll be here in the hour, Feather!" said Gaelyn, noticing her sister had stopped her polishing progress.

Gaelyn hardly couched her annoyance. Half a dozen of the town's most (self-proclaimed) distinguished ladies wouldn't either. If everything upon arrival wasn't a perfect expression of traditional values, their very best passive-aggressive disdain was sure to follow:

"Oh, you went with the tattered look, how quaint!"

"*I* could never be so bold as to adopt a devil-may-care attitude with *my* silver. You girls are so avant-garde!"

Gaelyn had always felt she had the potential to be dazzling. She wished she could reinvent her world, one in which she would host lively parties, enrobed in revealing, sequinned dresses that would hug her robust figure, offering thoughts on foreign politics over exotic and risqué-sounding drinks like Screaming Orgasm and Sex on the Beach. Sexy-sounding drinks might begin to make up for the lack of sex in her life.

Conversation over tea, on the other hand, was so soporific. Gaelyn had to dig her fingernails into her flesh to keep awake as her neighbours droned on about who could afford the latest car model, and who only pretended to. Every month, she ended up with tiny half-moon welts on her arms, souvenirs of the afternoon spent with the ladies of "good" families.

What galled Gaelyn further was that Feather genuinely seemed to enjoy conversing about the weather and the minister's latest sermon, and exchanging gossip about the lesser elements in town. Ugh, how those flashing eyes, eager for rumours, disgusted her. Feather's pointy nose and chin, more so than Gaelyn's for lack of fullness in the cheek, merely aggravated the look. Feather's was a face more familiar than her own — it was the one Gaelyn saw most, day in and day out.

Gaelyn wished for a confidante with whom to share her dreams of outrageousness, someone unashamed to wear bright oranges and reds, and silk scarves in her hair. She longed for a friendship that would pierce her life's tedium, a bond to help break all the tradition and convention.

∞

"There. It's done," said Feather, thunking the shined teapot down without regard for its lofty last-century provenance.

Feather stifled a sigh as she removed her rubber gloves. Gaelyn fiddled with her hair rollers and Feather shuddered.

"*Must* you do that in the kitchen? Heaven forbid anyone should find a greying hair on their scones."

Feather stood and turned on her heel without bothering to wait for her sister's reply. *She* would finish getting ready in her room, like a lady. Feather headed toward the main foyer and ascended the grand staircase. It was another point of contention with her sister, with its worn and treacherous pre-war carpet runner. She wanted it removed to reveal and refurbish the hardwood underneath, but Gaelyn insisted it be left untouched.

Moments later, adjusting her brassiere in the reflection of her vanity mirror, Feather sourly noticed her first white hair poking straight up from the top of her head.

"Fiddlesticks," she muttered, her inner self barely repressing a stronger oath. She leaned against the vanity, her arm brushing and nearly tipping an empty vase as she grimaced at her reflection.

She was so proud of her strawberry blond locks, especially since Gaelyn's had lost their lustre a few years back. Now that her hair was going the way of her sister's, it was mortifying. Feather didn't have time to drive to the store two towns over, where she could pick up a bottle of dye without being recognized. She would have to pluck the offending strand and hope more didn't show up for vengeance later.

She shimmied into her dress, struggling to zip up. At times like these, a husband would come in handy. Her thoughts turned to Jameson again, for which she chastised herself. Fresh out of school, certain she'd be engaged within months, she'd practiced saying "Feather and Jameson" and "Mrs. Feather Kinsley". She was glad she didn't know then that the refrain of her life would remain "Feather and Gaelyn"...

Feather stared at her reflection in the mirror and eased her hands from her neck to her breasts, stopping to rest at her hips. Feather once believed herself the most beautiful woman in the world, simply because he loved her. That was ancient history, dissolved in the summer heat, hazy memories the only remaining vestiges of that once-impenetrable confidence.

There were times when she dreamed of a more concrete legacy of their romance. In her wildest fantasies, which Feather seldom allowed herself, she imagined that she'd given birth to a love child. Though she'd never confided in anyone about hers and Jameson's intimate relations, Feather suspected her virginal sister had guessed that she'd allowed her beau to become her lover. But they'd never spoken about it. And there were days, infrequent yet affecting, when she wished that their liaison had borne a child, whether or not Jameson would have remained at her side. A child would have eased the loneliness she felt today, would have filled Hollingsworth Hall with giggles and squeals.

A husband, a child — Feather had had such hopes, such expectations. What had happened? Time slipped by her without so much as a cursory greeting and suddenly, here she was, a greying — ugh — spinster, hosting a tea with a reticent companion, in a rambling estate being sold off acre by acre. Soon, there would be nothing left but two Hollingsworth corpses in a pile of rubble on a patch of dried-up grass.

"Gaelyn!" shouted Feather from her bedroom door. "Come here!"

Feather waited as her sister made her way toward her, her heavy steps audible against the creaking floor.

∞

Hallway creaks were a staple of Feather and Gaelyn's childhood. As girls, they tried to scare one another with the most horrid and outlandish tales they could muster — rarely delving further than a scarecrow come to life or an axe murderer come to chop them to bits. As adolescents, they joked that the creaking outdated the house, and unsuccessfully attempted to bypass it when returning late from an evening out.

∞

"Zip."

Feather turned her back to Gaelyn, who grabbed the dainty zipper as if to do damage. But she shook her head and postponed delving into where these dark urges came from. Feather was her sister; she was obliged to love her. But, some days, Gaelyn's frustration squeezed upon her heart and she wished Feather would meet an unfortunate end on her way to one of the many outlet stores that threatened to overtake the town. And there were times, like this one, where she even imagined doing the deed herself. A strategically administered poison that would first affect Feather's looks, then her mind. Prescribed degeneration, Gaelyn's inner self smirked. The spectacle of Feather losing her hair, or wrinkling up, could be worth it. Prison couldn't be much worse than Hollingsworth Hell. Gaelyn shook her head free of the monstrousness again and zipped Feather's cream dress from mid-back to neck.

"Teatime!" she singsonged, a tone she scarcely adopted. "And remember, Mabel is bringing her sister this time. The youngest, Tallulah."

Gaelyn might have been pleased that her reminder of the guest list had cut Feather deeply. She might even have felt empathy for her sister, whose dreams of a happy ending with the man she loved were shot, as if the Tallulah in question had picked up her father's rifle and aimed directly at Feather's heart. But Gaelyn, who was often behind on gossip and news from town, was unaware of the effect of her words.

∞

Had Feather been able to sort through her feelings, she would have remembered that Gaelyn didn't yet know of Jameson's engagement and she could have perhaps stopped herself from lunging at her sister's throat, wishing she had a crumpet to cram down her gullet.

∞

"Fe-ghhgig...!" Gaelyn gulped for air, as she fell to the floor, trying to push her surprisingly sturdy sister off her.

Could Feather have guessed? How did she know that, just moments before, Gaelyn was imagining a poison of her own concoction gliding down her sister's throat, a delicious murder attempt to enliven her dreary existence? Was Feather picking up on these feelings — mere passing fancies, nothing more — and pre-empting the inevitable? Gaelyn's thoughts turned murky as her deoxygenated brain struggled to stay conscious.

∞

As her fingers began to ache from the strain of applying continued pressure on her sister's neck, Feather could feel the muscles in her own contract with effort. She blinked several times as if to see more clearly the effect of her labours on Gaelyn's distorted face beneath her, and hastily released her hands, staring at them as if they had acted on their own.

Gaelyn's pained gasps shook Feather back to the present moment, away from the force of fury that had inhabited her seconds before, away from the frustration and desperation of a life lived for no one but herself, away from the feeling that unless she choked the unspoken judgment out of Gaelyn's eyes, she would be stuck in this loveless limbo of an existence forever. Feather shook her head, surprised at herself. This was most unladylike behaviour.

∞

"What's the marghh— the matter with you?"

Gaelyn struggled from the bedroom floor.

"Oh, that's going to leave a mark," said Feather, getting up to pick a white daisy-printed scarf from her armoire and advancing toward Gaelyn with it.

"I've got it!" croaked Gaelyn, grabbing the scarf from her sister lest she attempt the strangulation again, this time with a flowery weapon.

"I don't know what came over me, Gaelyn, I apologize. It was most ill-mannered of me."

"Ill-mannered! It's criminal!"

"Criminal? A spat between sisters? Don't let us blow this out of proportion. I went too far and admitted it. You have to be the – ahem – bigger person and forgive me. I'm asking nicely."

∞

Gaelyn gently massaged her throat and winced at the pain. Forgive her sister? For trying to kill her? For absolutely no reason? Even though she had just been dreaming of doing the same?

"Come, Gaelyn, no dawdling!"

Gaelyn glanced at the vase on Feather's dresser and imagined, for a fraction of a second, bringing it down on Feather's head. It would be justified: self-defence. But she took a deep breath instead — as deep as her crushed windpipe would allow — and followed her sister downstairs without further incident.

As the Hollingsworth sisters descended the steps toward the main foyer to greet their imminent guests, Gaelyn felt less and less peeved by Feather's violent outburst. For all her dreams of glamour and intrigue, she was a proper lady, able to rise above the slightest insult and the most dreadful assault. She brought her hand to her neck again and stroked the fabric there. At least she got a scarf out of the affair — Gaelyn had always envied Feather's scarves.

∞

Careful to avoid the barest parts of the carpet on the stairs, where one would be apt to trip and fall, Feather and Gaelyn reached the foyer, not yet knowing that each would remain disappointed by her life while being secretly pleased her twin would fare no better. They did not yet know that their final competition —

whom would outlive the other — would be moot, the winner forever undeclared. They did not yet know that Tallulah Kinsley would care for them in their final days only a few years later, when, days apart, one suffering a stroke, the other falling down the grand staircase, fate left both Hollingsworth sisters in a quasi-vegetative state. They did not yet know that this was as good as it got.

∞

"I'll set the scones and such in the drawing room," said Gaelyn, turning toward the kitchen.

"I'll open the drapes," replied Feather.

"Did you dust them yesterday?"

"Yes. Did you know that there are new fabrics that don't require such constant upkeep?"

"You told me."

"Maybe we could look into that for the drawing room?"

"Our drawing room drapes are perfectly fine as they are. We'll discuss it again once they become beyond repair."

"The far east one has a tear in it; I told you that, too."

"Did you?"

The door knocker thudded heavily, announcing the first guests' arrival for tea.

"Feather, get the drapes. I'll get the door."

"But you'll think about it?"

"Fine. And get the scones, too."

Feather scurried away and Gaelyn warmly greeted Mabel and Tallulah.

WHERE PIGEONS ROOST

It was ironic that the game was based on the honour system. Mykle knew there was no honour in pigeon-thwacking, but she couldn't help herself. Whenever she made contact — and they were quick little buggers — she experienced a surge of satisfaction far outweighing any wisp of guilt.

As pigeon-thwacking was honour-based, one simply had to trust one's opponents to report the truth when notching a thwack. Mykle herself had abused the honour system only once, when a friend of her aunt's had brimmed with excitement with a story of how, after an invigorating tennis match, she'd come across a plump, arrogant specimen in the parking lot, too close to her Mercedes-Benz. She had dispatched it promptly with a well-placed volley of her PVC-clad tennis racket. Mykle, new to pigeon-thwacking, had pounced on the point, rationalizing that, as the woman was practically family and not in on the game herself, it was fair to record the exploit as her own.

Of course, it was exactly the opposite and *not* fair that she had allotted herself a higher score for a thwack she had not herself administered. And while none of her fellow players ever publicly doubted her total, Mykle's conscience was heavy until she herself volleyed a pair of pigeons, but only counted it as one.

Mykle's conscience and conscientiousness were at the root of her perpetual second-place standing in the overall regional thwacking rankings. She was a serious player, rarely missing a thwacking opportunity, but also preferring the challenge of thwacking younger, nimbler birds to the obvious win of bumping off the fatter Godfeathers. Resolved never again to repeat her scoring indiscretion, Mykle sought to be an honourable player. There were rumblings that Toyosi, the reigning champion, was inflating his numbers, but nothing could be proven.

Counting points in pigeon-thwacking is a simple matter. One thwack equals one point. For the point to count, contact has to be made between the player and the pigeon, either directly — such as a well-placed kick — or indirectly, through any blunt instrument wielded by the player — such as a rock or a bat. Extra points can be earned by arguing their merit with one's opponents, and only upon the approval of the latter. Mykle once tried to get additional points for when she thwacked a trio of pigeons with a car, arguing that the exploit was meritorious because pigeons are usually adept at avoiding vehicles, but while her fellow players had been impressed, some, including Toyosi, had countered that a thwack with such a large surface was hardly exceptional. Mykle had accepted the verdict, but suspected that Toyosi was ensuring he kept her total inferior to his.

Each game cycle lasted a year. While most of it was dedicated to independent play, there were seasonal meets for the diehard fans of the game, usually attended by recreational thwackists rather than by serious contenders. Mykle showed up when she could.

At the meets, she would field questions from enthusiasts, captivating them with tales of particularly-pleasing pigeon-thwacks and of the rare shrewd but agonizing pigeon escape. The thwackists also discussed pigeon habits — where flocks ate, where they roosted — and thwacking strategies. Most fans, and even some players, made the mistake, Mykle believed, of going for the kill when thwacking, even though extra points were rarely added for pigeon deaths. To Mykle, a pigeon that flew post-thwack was a pigeon vulnerable to being thwacked again.

In her early days in the game, while researching her prey, Mykle had read somewhere online that, when dying of natural causes, pigeons preferred to die alone, crawling into vents or other tight spaces, where they would be less vulnerable to their predators and a more gruesome final fate. At first, Mykle sought out these dying birds — easy thwacking prey — but quickly tired of searching abandoned buildings or roof corners for the proverbial sitting ducks.

If Mykle had harboured any reservations about joining the game, they were quickly replaced by the thrill of the thwack. It was a feeling incomprehensible to the anti-thwack movement. The research, strategy, and execution of carefully-planned thwacks was, to them, tantamount to avicide. They gave no weight to the argument that thwackists helped control the city's pigeon population. Ultimately, their pleas to the authorities went unheeded. There were many worse crimes to investigate and, in any case, the anti-thwackists had to counter ridicule at their claims of an underground, inhumane pigeon hunt.

This, of course, was due to the unspoken rule that thwacking in public — the regular, uninitiated public — was discouraged. Not only did this starve the anti-thwackists of ammunition, it also kept the game to the thrilling terrain of insiders alone.

Mykle failed to understand the appeal of protecting pigeons. They served no useful purpose, and had few natural predators. They were unattractive, pesky scavengers, highly deserving the epithet of "flying rodents". A good thwack served them well, she thought.

She knew that some people still ate pigeons, though she wondered about the edibility of city pigeons, whose diets included copious amounts of garbage. They were also potential carriers of the West Nile virus and salmonella, neither of which could be covered

up by Shake 'n Bake or béchamel sauce. Mykle
had tried pigeon once, at a touristy bistro, a few
hours from the city. She'd been surprised by the
squab's pleasant aroma, and by the fine texture
and tenderness of the dainty, dark meat. She
had considered thwacking for the kill more often
to save on grocery bills a few times a month,
but she had grown too intimate with the
pigeons, seen too many of their scavenging
habits to bring her prey home, pluck its
feathers, smother it in sauce, and set it in the
oven to roast.

And so Mykle thwacked for the pleasure
of it.

She was determined that Toyosi would
not hold on to his title. It was something she
promised herself every year since his ascent to
rank of champion. This time around, she was
more discreet about her training regimen,
hoping to surprise her opponents — and
especially her nemesis — with her total at the
final count. Opponents with similar counts – that
is, within 20 thwacks – forced a tiebreaker
challenge. Anticipating her chance at
redemption this year, Mykle could already hear
the amassed crowd of hundreds of fans
cheering her on, huddled between the load-

bearing pillars of the "abandoned" building —
usually a hangar rented for the occasion —
around the netted "thwackrena" where the last
battle of the year would be held.

Set up by retired champions, these
battles consist of two dozen pigeons set loose
in the netting, with the top contenders and their
one weapon of choice. They last for a period of
forty minutes or until all the birds are dead,
whichever comes first. The contender
administering the most thwacks within those
limits wins the year's championship. In Mykle's
opinion, there was little sport in thwacking
caged birds, but tradition was tradition.

One had to be strategic in the
thwackrena. A fatal thwack robbed one's
opponent of further thwacks, but it also robbed
oneself of potential catch-up thwacks if one fell
behind in the totals. One's choice of weapon
was also key. It could be advantageous if one
was quick to thwack with a hand-wielded
weapon, but the pigeons quickly caught on and
flew to the far reaches of the netting, where a
projectile weapon could mean the difference
between earning the title and returning home in
perpetual second place.

While Mykle was hopeful that her total would automatically win her this year's title, last year's thwackrena final yielded one insight: a window into Toyosi's thwacking technique. Mykle's pre-final total had forced a battle the year before, spotlighting her agile skill versus Toyosi's scavenging habit of targeting wounded birds. It was only her choice of weapon — a tennis racket, in reminiscence of the false point she had claimed years earlier — that cost her the game's championship.

Toyosi's weapon had proved more effective, despite Mykle's attempts at discarding his ammunition outside the net. His slingshot had thwacked all the Mykle-wounded pigeons to death — save one feisty fellow — in a bid to minimize Mykle's thwacking opportunities. With their scores neck-and-neck, she lunged for the final bird, managing contact on the tip of its tail with the tip of her racket. Mykle was ahead with just a few minutes remaining on the clock. She only had to block Toyosi's access to the pigeon until the game ran out, or kill the pigeon herself.

The second scenario had seemed almost certain. Mykle, keeping an eye on the exhausted pigeon, hanging from the top of the netting by its toes, also caught Toyosi's

33

movement in her peripheral vision. He was aiming his slingshot at the pigeon, and Mykle refused to allow him a thwack. She shouted out, but his concentration did not waver. Desperate, Mykle ululated. Half-wail, half-battle cry, the shrill howl pierced the fans' cheers. Startled by the strident sound, Toyosi winced, his carefully-aimed shot missing its target. Toyosi's final stone hit the netting and fell among the pigeon carcasses. He was now out of ammunition.

Mykle seized her chance. The pigeon, dislodged from its perch by the rock that whizzed past its head, flew downward. Mykle readied herself and lobbed, the pigeon's pained squawk drowned by the crowd's roar of approval.

The pigeon, stunned, careened up into the air, then plunged down again, unable to adjust its course. Mykle positioned herself for the smash that would likely finish off the bird and end the game, when two pigeons — the one at which she had been aiming and suddenly another — sailed overhead and landed with a thud behind her. The crowd screamed even louder and a siren rang out, announcing the end of the game.

Mykle, baffled that Toyosi had robbed her of her final thwack, was still confident of her win, until the judges declared that extra points were being allotted to Toyosi for having used a pigeon as slingshot ammunition to thwack another pigeon.

The crowd erupted again, an even mix of cheers and boos. Mykle's fans shouted out accusations of cheating, and artificial inflation of Toyosi's qualifying numbers. Toyosi's defenders retorted that to question someone's honour in the game was dishonourable, and Mykle was simply a poor loser — perhaps even a poor player. As thwackist fans began shoving each other, Mykle knew she had to intervene. Twenty-four pigeon deaths was tally enough for the evening; she didn't want to add human injury to the list. She asked for the microphone and addressed the rowdy crowd.

"Fellow thwackists, we thank you for your enthusiasm! A final battle always brings out the thwacking in us, doesn't it?"

The crowd laughed and the squabbling petered out.

"We have just witnessed a terrific championship battle. Thwacks made here tonight will surely go down in thwackist history."

The fans hooted in approval.

"I, for one, am already planning my next thwacking foray, and invite you to do the same. Perhaps one of you will be battling it out in the thwackrena next year! In that case — I will see you there!"

Again, the crowd roared its approval and began chanting "Mykle! Mykle!" despite Toyosi being the champion. It felt like a victory of honour, and that, she savoured.

Despite her speech, Mykle's plan was *not* to face anyone in the thwackrena this year. Her total would so surpass those of her adversaries that no final battle would be necessary.

For the past ten-and-a-half months, Mykle had concentrated most of her free time on the game. Even her annual vacation had been thwacking-oriented; she visited the ultimate pigeons' roost: Piazza San Marco in Venice. Despite the many witnesses, she ensured a fair amount of contact through slaps and kicks, the pigeons returning for more, lured by breadcrumbs Mykle tossed their way.

So far, Mykle's total was nearly 50 per cent above that of last year, but she still felt that she could add to it. Who knew by how much Toyosi would inflate his total? She had to compensate for that, without cheating.

Mykle set up an array of makeshift roosting platforms on the roofs of the buildings surrounding hers by setting down planks of wood sheltered from the sunlight and scattering seeds generously around them. It wasn't long before flocks of pigeons came to roost. Mykle went to each rooftop twice a day, where she administered a mild thwacking to each flock, enough to allot herself thwacking points, but not so hard as to frighten the birds away. The sport was gone from the game, but victory would finally be hers.

She had brought her old tennis racket with her that morning, to begin the day with a thwack of a few birds. The soft coo of the pigeon cocks greeted her as she arrived on the roof. Mykle suddenly understood how rookie thwackists who grew to feel compassion or even love for their bred or caged pigeons became unable to continue playing. Despite the sudden burst of sentiment for her winged companions, she refocused on her championship goal, and raised her racket to administer a multiple thwack, as she had on so many occasions over the past few months. Yet this time, the pigeons seemed ready for the assault. They flew up, en masse, in a clatter of flapping wings, surprising Mykle mid-swing. The momentum caused her to slip on a spot of bird droppings and, unable to catch herself, Mykle hit her head with a dull and heavy "thwack" on the concrete roof. She lost consciousness.

The sun was high above when she came to, her left eye and cheek encrusted in blood. She tried to rise, but was unable to move. The throbbing pain in her skull was intense and made her feel nauseated.

"Help!" she managed to croak out. "Help!"

Only the pigeons could hear her. She lost consciousness again.

It was evening when she awoke, still prostrate, on the concrete roof. Mykle knew this was the end. Brought low by pigeons. She was less distraught by the thought of dying than by the thought of winning the pigeon-thwacking championship without anyone ever knowing about it. With the little strength she had left, Mykle lifted her right index finger and dipped it in the congealed pool of blood under her face. And she painstakingly etched out, blood smear by blood smear, the numbers 2-2-1-5-8 on the ground next to her.

In the dimming sunlight, she could just make out a grey-green pigeon staring at her with its beady red eyes. If she had been able to, she would have given it a good kick. As it was, she managed a flick of her bloodied hand, and the bird flapped its wings. Its coo was the last thing Mykle heard as she plunged into darkness one final time.

Photo by Danielle Maheu

ABOUT THE AUTHOR

Award-winning author and playwright A.M. Matte was first published at age 11.

Laureate of the O'Neill-Karch award, she writes in English and in French. Her plays have been produced across Ontario.

Previous publications include *Son of Sun* in *North of Infinity II*, and *Secrets*, *À l'air*, and *Nelles* in *Virages*.

A.M. Matte lives in Toronto with her husband, her son, and her bird, who has never been thwacked.

www.ingramcontent.com/pod-product-compliance
Lightning Source LLC
Chambersburg PA
CBHW071352130626
46556CB00005B/2146